QREADS

NO WAY
TO RUN

JANICE GREENE

SADDLEBACK
EDUCATIONAL PUBLISHING

▉QREADS

SADDLEBACK
EDUCATIONAL PUBLISHING
www.sdlback.com

ISBN-13: 978-1-61651-184-5
ISBN-10: 1-61651-184-2
eBook: 978-1-60291-906-8

Printed in the U.S.A.

21 20 19 18 17   6 7 8 9 10

■ ■ ■

Darn!" Jasmine muttered under her breath. The business card she'd been holding had slipped from her fingers and fallen under the desk. Making sure her wheelchair was locked, she pushed forward on the seat and slowly slid down to the floor. Her useless legs folded under her.

She snatched up the card and began to pull herself back onto her chair. Then she looked out the door to see if anyone was watching. She hated for anyone to see how helpless she was. But Patty and Shauna were busy with customers. And it was near the end of the day. Soon they'd be taking the watches and necklaces and earrings and bracelets from the display cases. De Lanza Jewelers would be closed for the night.

Jasmine went back to her computer, entering suppliers' names in neat rows. She tried not to yawn. Accounting wasn't work she loved, but it paid the rent. In fact she was very grateful to have her job. Most employers wouldn't consider hiring people who were paralyzed from the waist down.

She hardly noticed when the door chimed and someone walked in. Last-minute customers were not unusual. But then she heard a sound—half-gasp, half-sob—that made her scalp prickle.

Peering through the window at the front showroom, Jasmine saw a man in a ski mask standing close to Shauna! He poked a pistol with a long extension—a silencer, she knew from TV—into the girl's ribs. Her hands shaking, Shauna opened a display case.

Jasmine stared at the phone on her desk. "Move!" she told herself. "Call 911!" But she was frozen, helpless.

There was a click as the display case opened. Then the man shoved Shauna aside and neatly swept a pile of jewelry into his backpack. But just then Patty made a slight noise as she reached under the counter. Jasmine knew exactly what she was doing. That's where the silent alarm was hidden!

The man whirled around. Patty jerked her hand away from the counter, her eyes wide with terror. He knew what she'd done! The man aimed the gun and fired. There was a muffled pop. Then Jasmine saw a dark stain spread across the center of Patty's blouse before the wounded woman crumpled to the floor.

The man turned and hurried to the door, pulling off his ski mask. But just as his face was revealed, he glanced into the back office and saw Jasmine!

For a long moment, she stared at the light blue eyes and the cleft chin in his narrow face. He stared back fiercely, and Jasmine felt as exposed as if she were naked. Then suddenly he was gone.

Jasmine turned to Shauna. She was bent over the counter, as if holding herself up. Her body shook with sobs.

Jasmine wheeled over to her quickly. "Move it, Shauna! Go check Patty's breathing," she said. "I'll call 911."

"Her breathing?" Shauna's voice was little more than a whimper.

"Tip her head back a little," said Jasmine. "Then put your ear next to her mouth. Tell me if you can feel any air coming out."

Shauna bent over Patty and did as she was told. "I can't feel anything!" she cried. "Jasmine—she's *dead!*" In panic, Shauna's hands fluttered to her face.

Jasmine grabbed Shauna's wrist. "Calm down!" she ordered. "You're going to check her pulse now."

Shauna pulled away. "I can't touch her! She's—she's *dead,* Jasmine!"

"Get the phone and do what I tell you," Jasmine ordered. Then she slid onto the floor and pulled herself over to Patty. The young woman had a weak pulse, but she wasn't breathing at all.

Shauna called 911 while Jasmine began rescue breathing.

By the time the paramedics arrived, Jasmine's neck ached and her upper body was shaking with exhaustion.

Quickly, the two young men lifted Patty onto a stretcher. "Will she make it?" Jasmine asked.

"I can't tell until we have a look at her," the man nearest her said sternly. Then he noticed Jasmine's empty wheelchair and his look softened. Smiling, he patted Jasmine on the shoulder. "Good for you—you did all right," he said.

Jasmine heard the harsh wail of more sirens. Then two police officers walked in. Jasmine's heart sank. She longed to be out of the store. More than anything, she wanted to close her eyes and never look at this place again.

■ ■ ■

One officer sat down with Shauna, another with Jasmine, and the questions began. "Tell us what you remember about the shooter, Ms. Deang," the officer said to Jasmine.

"He was kind of tall," she said. "At least five foot ten. He had long, thin arms and really white skin. His hair was short on the sides and long and spiky on top. He wore navy blue gloves."

The officer smiled slightly. "You'd recognize him in a line-up?" he asked.

"I'd recognize that guy *anywhere,*" Jasmine said confidently. She was certain she'd never forget that face.

Jasmine left the store three hours later than usual. Waiting for the bus in the growing darkness, she watched for the gunman. She half expected him to come around every corner. On the long ride home, she watched every new passenger who got on the bus.

The robbery replayed over and over in her mind. How surprised she was at the way Shauna and Patty had acted! Shauna was usually *bold*. She went to dances and clubs alone. She sassed impatient customers and flirted with men she liked—even if they were shopping for engagement rings. Yet Shauna had fallen apart in an emergency! It had been Patty—shy, quiet Patty—who'd been brave enough to push the alarm. Patty was afraid of birds and horses and loud noises. She wilted when customers were rude. But Patty had been the one to risk her life. It was something to think about.

"Third Street!" the driver called. It was Jasmine's stop. As she wheeled down the sidewalk toward home, she looked around anxiously. But the street was deserted. Jasmine lived in a cottage at the back of a house belonging to a large family, the Forresters. Sometimes the noisy family got on Jasmine's nerves. Tonight she would have been glad to hear their loud TV and barking dog. But they were off camping somewhere, and the house was dark and silent.

As she opened the door, Spanky jumped in front of her chair, meowing loudly. Her cat was obviously outraged that she was home so late.

"I'm sorry, Spanky. I'm *sooo* sorry," said Jasmine. For a special treat she gave him a can of tuna.

Too tired to eat anything herself, she watched while he ate. When he finished, the big cat jumped onto her lap, purring noisily.

As she stroked his fur, Jasmine began to cry. She cried and cried until Spanky finally jumped off her lap and shook himself.

"Oh, I got you wet!" said Jasmine.

Spanky gave her such an offended look that Jasmine laughed in spite of herself. Spanky was a comfort.

She wheeled though the kitchen and into the bedroom. The house was dead quiet. Wanting to hear a human voice, she phoned Ben, hoping it wasn't a mistake.

"Hi," she said.

"What's wrong?" Ben demanded. He could

always tell instantly when something was bothering her.

Jasmine told him about the robbery.

"It's like I was frozen!" said Jasmine. "The phone was right there on my desk, and I couldn't call 911."

"Maybe your instincts told you it was too dangerous," said Ben. "*You* could've been shot instead of Patty."

"But I was just *helpless,* Ben! I couldn't even make a move to save her," Jasmine cried out bitterly.

"Jasmine—just listen to what you're saying! You gave her mouth-to-mouth!" said Ben. "You're too hard on yourself."

"You always say that," said Jasmine.

"Yeah, well—you sound really tired," said Ben. "Why don't I come over? I'll watch TV and stand guard while you sleep. I'll make sure you're safe."

Jasmine felt slightly annoyed. "Ben, I don't need your protection," she said. "The police know where I live. They'll be patrolling the neighborhood."

"Then how about I come over just to give you some company?" he asked.

"No, it's too late, Ben. I'm just about to go to bed," said Jasmine.

"What about tomorrow?" he said.

"Why don't you give it a rest, Ben? You just keep pushing!" she said.

"And *you* keep retreating! Come on, Jasmine! Why won't you let me spend time with you?" said Ben.

"Because I know it won't work!" she said in an exasperated voice.

"You're just so sure it won't work out," said Ben. "You won't even give me a chance! Is that fair?"

"You want *fair*?" Jasmine cried bitterly. "Nothing is fair in this life!" She slammed down the phone. Now she felt more angry than tired. Her nerves felt wired. She knew it would be a long time before she fell asleep tonight.

She pictured Ben's warm brown eyes and slow smile. She wondered what it would be like to kiss him. Then she pictured Ben with another woman—the two of them racing down a sunny sidewalk. That's the way it would be in the end. Why should she kid herself? And why should *he* be so unrealistic? He wouldn't stay, she *knew* it.

■ ■ ■

Just as Jasmine had done a thousand times, she relived the accident that had crippled her. She remembered Christmas music playing on the radio and the wet pavement reflecting the colored lights at the entrance to the mall. She had just pulled out of the parking lot and onto the expressway. Then suddenly she had been hit from behind! She'd never seen the car coming.

There was an enormous *thud* as the impact propelled her car forward, ramming it into the car in front of her. Then she heard crushing, tearing sounds as her little car collapsed like a flimsy crumpled bag between the other two. Just inches from her face, she saw webs of cracking glass spreading across the windshield.

Jasmine had been pinned under the dashboard. Slowly, carefully, rescue workers had pulled her out. At first, she thought she'd been lucky. Only her chest and shoulders hurt from smacking against the seatbelt and the steering wheel. But when her body was finally free, she realized she couldn't get up.

"Something's wrong with my legs," she said with growing horror. "I can't feel my legs! *I can't feel my legs!*"

The memory of that heartbreaking discovery still brought bitter tears.

After the accident there were hours and hours of physical therapy at the hospital. Every day she discovered one more thing she couldn't do. She cried with frustration when she couldn't do simple tasks like making a bed. Small jobs she'd done all her life were suddenly overwhelming.

Then came the wheelchair—the ugly machine that made her feel trapped and set her apart from normal people.

There was no one to blame for the accident except the man who'd hit her—

and it was too late for that. He'd been killed instantly when his car smashed hers. But in her frustration, Jasmine had lashed out at everyone who came near. She swore at doctors, nurses, and physical therapists—especially when they tried to be kind. Her black moods drove away her girlfriends and her boyfriend, Don. In the end, only her mom and dad and her brother, Kip, remained. They had simply refused to be driven away. Not once had they said, "We understand." They hadn't promised that everything was going to be okay. That helped. Once, her father had told her, "The way you deal with your disability is the biggest decision you'll ever have to make, Jasmine."

"What do you mean?" she had asked.

"You can use your disability as an excuse to give up," he said, "—to stop struggling for the things you want in life. *Or* you can insist that it's not going to get in your way—and struggle even harder to achieve your goals. It's your choice."

She'd yelled at him for saying that. "This isn't a *life,* Dad! I might as well be dead! I wish I was dead!"

But she was alive—and slowly she became glad that she'd survived. She was proud when she was able to get in and out of her wheelchair without help. It pleased her to accomplish small tasks, like making breakfast, on her own. As she learned to accept what had happened, she stopped yelling at doctors and nurses. She asked for advice and took their help when she needed it.

Finally, after many months, Jasmine was ready to leave the hospital. Her parents helped her find the place behind the Forresters'. Kip hung cabinets she could reach and lowered the sink and counter to her level. For company, Mom brought her a kitten, Spanky.

Slowly, Jasmine rejoined the noisy, bustling world. After a long search, she found a job. She started playing basketball and found friends on the court. Then she'd signed up for night classes to work toward her college degree. That's where she'd met Ben.

At first he'd been nothing more than a pal. They helped each other with assignments. He laughed at her jokes. Once they'd almost been kicked out of the library because he laughed so hard at her comic impersonation of a teacher clearing his throat.

Then Ben started trying to get closer. He asked about her old boyfriends. Then he asked her out on a date.

"I'm not ready, Ben," she told him. But in her heart she wondered if she would *ever* be ready. The confidence that she'd been building seemed like a thin tower. If Ben got close—and then rejected her—the tower would crash to the ground. So she had gently pushed Ben away, and it had angered him.

■ ■ ■

Jasmine sat up and looked at the clock—12:30. She was tired now, but her brain refused to shut down. She called the hospital. Patty was in critical but stable condition, they said. "Hang in there, Patty," Jasmine said softly as she hung up the phone. Then she dropped onto the pillow and finally drifted off.

Early the next morning, Saturday, Jasmine awoke with a groan. There was nothing to look forward to this weekend but laundry and house cleaning. The only bright spot was basketball practice. Her team, the Flaming Wheels, practiced two hours every Sunday afternoon.

All weekend long, the thought of returning to work loomed like a dark cloud in the distance. She wished she could quit. She never wanted to go back to De Lanza Jewelers again.

Monday morning came all too soon. Shauna showed up on time, very quiet but calm. Jasmine left her bookkeeping chores and did what she could to help her. She'd never dealt with the public before. But to Jasmine's surprise, she actually enjoyed showing customers the beautiful jewelry and watches. She sold a pretty bracelet to an older man and helped him plan a way to surprise his wife with it.

"You could put it someplace where she'd be sure to see it," said Jasmine. "Someplace that's part of her routine."

"Good idea!" said the man. "I always bring her coffee in bed in the morning. I'll fasten it to the mug handle!" As he laughed delightedly, Jasmine felt a painful pang of envy. She was sure that no one would ever love her like that.

That afternoon, as she was getting on the bus, something caught her eye. A man standing near the bus stop was wearing a knit cap, even though it was a hot day. Then she noticed how long and pale his arms were. Fear gripped her chest like a huge, cold hand.

"Excuse me," a woman's voice said. Jasmine moved to get out of the woman's way. When she looked again, the strange man had disappeared.

The bus lumbered away. Was it really the thief she had seen? She couldn't be sure. She longed to get to the back of the bus and see if he was following in a car. But the walkway between the aisles was solidly packed with people. She gritted her teeth in frustration.

Jasmine considered getting off at a different stop—but what difference would it make? If he was out there, he could follow her, no matter what. She remembered how fast she used to run. In those days, she could have gotten off at a different stop and easily snaked through the park to get to her house. She could have lost him for sure.

"Stop it!" she told herself. Those days were gone, lost in the car accident. Today she had only her arms—and her brain. She must use them as best she could.

Jasmine got off the bus and quickly sped down the sidewalk toward home. The cottage was two blocks away. One block ran along a row of houses. At the corner was a convenience store. The next block bordered a park. One side of the walk was thick with bushes and trees and laced with jogging trails.

Jasmine glanced around as she passed

in front of the houses. Two cars passed by. A woman came out of the convenience store. Then a black pickup drove slowly down the street, as if looking for a parking place. But why? There were plenty of empty spaces. Jasmine peered at the driver. All she could see was the dim silhouette of a head and shoulders. Was the driver wearing a cap? It looked like it, but she couldn't be sure. She wheeled faster, beads of sweat forming on her forehead. She passed the convenience store. Maybe she could wait in there—but for how long? An hour? Three hours? She shook her head. No, that would just make it worse. She wanted to be home. So she wheeled on, hoping she hadn't made a mistake.

Jasmine crossed the side street bordering the park. Often, on her way home, she was passed by joggers. But today the sidewalk was deserted, its long stretch of concrete shadowed by trees.

A vehicle came up beside her. It was the black pickup! She pushed the wheels of her chair faster, faster. Her heart was racing. If only she could leap out of her chair and take off running!

Behind her, she heard the truck stop, its motor still running. She pushed her wheels frantically, panting with effort. Her arms began to ache, and rivers of sweat trickled down her cheeks.

She heard heavy footsteps behind her.

Suddenly, a man's hand holding a knife was thrust in front of her face. The five-inch blade was so close she could see her breath on it. "Don't say *nothin'*!" the man hissed.

■ ■ ■

Jasmine grabbed the man's knife hand. *"Police!"* she screamed.

"Shut up!" he hissed. Then he swung at her. But Jasmine quickly ducked and backed up the chair, trying to run the wheels over his foot.

"Hey!" he yelled as he furiously struck out and slapped her cheek.

Then suddenly, from the trees just ahead

of them, a man and woman in running clothes burst out onto the sidewalk.

"Help!" Jasmine yelled.

The joggers ran over to her. Wheeling around, Jasmine saw her assailant racing back to his truck. In a split second, he gunned the motor and sped out of sight.

"Thank you!" Jasmine cried out to her rescuers in a shaky voice.

"Did anyone get the license number?" the woman asked.

"Part of it was *CFG*," Jasmine said.

"Are you sure? I thought it was *CFC*," said the man.

The woman looked at Jasmine sympathetically. "Are you okay? Can we call the police for you? I have my cell phone in the car," she said.

"That's what I'm going to do the minute I get home," said Jasmine.

"Is your home nearby?" the man asked. "We'll walk along with you."

Jasmine tried to hurry—but the block was a long one, and she was hot and tired.

As she said goodbye to the couple, she thought she heard a noise near the fence. She wondered if the thief could already have driven around the block and tracked her here.

When she was alone, Jasmine listened at the door to the cottage. But the only sound she could hear was the rustle of leaves in the hot breeze. Shaking her head, she went inside.

Then, with Spanky in her lap, Jasmine wheeled through the house, locking and bolting the doors. In spite of the heat, she decided to close the windows, too. The heavy screens as well as the glass would help to protect her. "Off you go, Spanky," she said, dumping the cat from her lap as she reached into the closet. To help her close the windows, Kip had made her a long wooden pole with a hook on top.

She'd closed the last window when she heard a faint noise outside. What was it? The drainpipe? Was he climbing up the drainpipe? She waited, listening, frozen in her chair.

Then she heard tiptoeing footsteps on the roof. A cold wave of fear washed over her.

The skylight in the living room—she'd forgotten to close it! She headed for the living room, the pole in one hand.

She heard a creak from above and looked up. A hand—*his* hand—was forcing the skylight open wider! Jasmine grabbed the pole in both hands and hit him on the knuckles—hard.

"Auuuugh!" he bellowed. Then the man's face appeared, and she was chilled by the determination in his light blue eyes. A few drops of his blood dripped down on her forehead.

She swung the pole again. When the man tried to grab it, she managed to whack his wrist. He howled in pain.

But then he grabbed the pole. Before she could tighten her grip, he pulled it out of her hands. She quickly wheeled around and sped out of the room.

As she passed through her bedroom, Jasmine grabbed the phone and punched in

911. As soon as a voice answered, she said, *"Hurry! He's in the house!"* Then she threw the phone under the bed, hoping the call could be traced.

The next thing she heard was a heavy thump as the man dropped through the skylight and landed on the floor.

She wheeled into the kitchen and pulled open the cabinet under the sink. Reaching in as far as she could without falling out of her chair, Jasmine grabbed a can of insect spray. She set it between her legs. Then she opened a drawer and took out a roll of duct tape. After pulling an inch of tape free, she shoved the roll up her arm like a bracelet.

■ ■ ■

Then the kitchen door banged open and the man was there, the knife in his hand. He charged, the blade flashing in a ray of light from the kitchen window. Jasmine let him come closer before she lifted the spray can and pressed the button. He swerved and grabbed her wrist—but not soon enough. The spray misted over the left half of his head, drenching his ear, eye, and open mouth. *"Augggh!"* he yelled. A nasty-sweet odor filled the room. Jasmine flung the spray can on top of the refrigerator.

The man swung at Jasmine's neck with the knife, but she grabbed his wrist. Then he went for her neck with his free hand, but she was able to grab it first. Frustrated, he pushed against her and slammed her wheelchair against the counter.

Now the man's face was inches away. One eye was closed. He was gagging and drooling from the blast of insect spray. Then he spit at her. "You're gonna pay for this, sister!" he screamed in her face. "You're gonna pay!"

Jasmine held his wrist and hand. Weakened by the dose of poisonous spray, the man struggled but could not break free. Jasmine pushed with all her might—and slowly, slowly, she forced him back. More than a year of wheeling the chair and playing basketball had paid off. She was *strong!*

Jasmine could feel the man's arms quivering with effort. She knew he was tiring. Still holding on to him, she shook her arm until the duct tape dropped to her wrist.

Holding onto his knife hand, she let go of his other hand to yank loose a length of tape. His free hand struck her hard on the jaw, and the pain filled her whole head. But as he drew his arm back for another blow, she quickly looped the tape over his wrist. He tried to jerk away to free himself, but Jasmine quickly pulled the tape over his knife hand. The man swore and swung his arms wildly. But every time he moved, she was able to wrap more tape around his wrists and hands.

There was a loud banging on the front door. *"Help!"* she yelled. *"I'm here!"*

It was the police. In seconds, they pulled away her assailant and handcuffed him. His face was blotchy and red from the insect spray. His nose was running, and one eye was swollen shut. Looking beaten and exhausted, the man stumbled as he was led away.

Two officers listened to her story, one asking questions while the other scribbled notes. When she described her battle with the intruder, the police officers looked at her first with surprise and then with respect. Jasmine felt a glow of accomplishment and pride.

Within a few minutes, a reporter and a cameraman from a local TV station showed up. While the glassy eye of the camera stared at Jasmine, the newscaster gushed, "You are truly a remarkable young lady. It's amazing that someone in a wheelchair could fend off a vicious killer the way you did."

"Well, sure," Jasmine said modestly. "It's not like I'm *helpless!*"

An hour or so later Jasmine was finally alone. She wheeled into the bedroom and noticed a fat lump in the middle of the bed. She lifted the bedspread and said, "Come on out, scaredy cat. Everyone's gone." Spanky crawled out and jumped in her lap.

Jasmine reached for the phone and called the hospital. A nurse said that Patty was stable, but still in critical condition.

Jasmine prayed that Patty's spine had not been injured. If so, that unfortunate young woman could end up in a wheelchair, too. At one time Jasmine had thought she'd be better off dead than stuck forever in a wheelchair. But now she had a life—and she knew that her life was going to be okay.

After a moment's pause, she punched in another number. And just as she had expected, she heard a recording. She knew that Ben had a science class tonight. "Hi," Jasmine said, "it's me. I just called to say—I just wanted to say—*Yes.* Yes, I want to see you. I want you to come over. I want to go out with you, Ben. Give me a call."

Then Jasmine wheeled into the living room and looked for just the right CD. She wanted something fast and loud. Tomorrow she'd start looking for a new job—something challenging, something she'd *love* to do.

Taking a deep, shaky breath, she shoved in the CD and began to dance. Maybe what she was doing wouldn't *look* like much of a dance to most people—but it was to her. She gracefully moved her head and arms and shoulders to the beat. Somehow the music had never sounded sweeter than it did right now.

After-Reading Wrap-Up

1. Is *No Way to Run* a good title for the story? Explain why or why not.

2. After spraying the intruder's face with bug killer, why did Jasmine throw the can on top of the refrigerator?

3. Contrast Jasmine's outlook on life after the accident with her outlook at the beginning of the story.

4. Why did Jasmine refuse to go out with Ben?

5. After calling 911, why did Jasmine throw the phone under the bed?

6. At the end of the story, Jasmine had made two decisions. What were they?